# It HURTS When I Poop!

To all of my patients who have had poop problems
over the years – HJB

To the memory of Moose, Debo Johnson,
Susie, and Chopper – MSW

Published by
MAGINATION PRESS
An Educational Publishing Foundation Book
American Psychological Association
750 First Street, NE
Washington, DC 20002

For more information about our books, including a complete catalog, please write to us,
call 1-800-374-2721, or visit our website at www.maginationpress.com.

Printed by Worzalla, Stevens Point, Wisconsin

Library of Congress Cataloging-in-Publication Data

Bennett, Howard J.
It hurts when I poop! : A story for children who are scared to use the potty /
by Howard J. Bennett ; illustrated by M.S. Weber.
p. cm.
ISBN-13: 978-1-4338-0130-3 (hardcover : alk. paper)
ISBN-10: 1-4338-0130-2 (hardcover : alk. paper)
ISBN-13: 978-1-4338-0131-0 (pbk. : alk. paper)
ISBN-10: 1-4338-0131-0 (pbk. : alk. paper)
1. Constipation in children—Juvenile literature. I. Weber, M. S. (Michael S.) II. Title.
RJ456.C76B46 2007
618.92'3428—dc22                                                  2007008760

10 9 8 7 6

ECO-FRIENDLY BOOKS
Made in the USA

# It HURTS When I Poop!

## A Story for Children
## Who Are Scared to Use the Potty

written by Howard J. Bennett, M.D.
illustrated by M.S. Weber

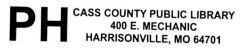
MAGINATION PRESS • WASHINGTON, DC

**R**yan loved playing with his dinosaurs.
They chased each other across the plains,
down into craters, and through the forest.

All of a sudden, Ryan got a tummy ache.

It felt like someone was poking him with a stick.

Ryan knew why his tummy hurt.

He had a poop inside that needed to come out.

He did not like having poops,

because it hurt when he tried to go.

When Ryan got tummy aches, he squeezed his bottom muscles as hard as he could to make the poop go away. This worked for a while, but somehow the feeling always came back. Then Ryan could not hold his poop in any longer, and it would come out.

Sometimes it came out as hard little balls.
Other times it came out as one big ball.

Sometimes Ryan had his poops on the potty.
But most of the time he was too scared to sit on the potty, and he asked his mom or dad for a pull-up.

Ryan's parents worried about him when he had tummy aches.
They told him he would feel better if the poop came out.
Ryan wanted his parents to be happy with him,
but he remembered that it hurt if he had a big poop.
So most of the time he tried to keep the poop in.

One day Ryan's parents
took him to see the doctor.
After Dr. Gold heard
about the tummy aches
and gave Ryan a check-up,
she told him a story about
a coyote named Bill.

When Bill was little, his mom and dad taught him to clean up after himself. He loved picking up trash, and once a week a big garbage truck came to take the trash away. This kept the house clean from top to bottom.

Now that Bill was older, he lived by himself.
Although he was a good worker and a good friend,
he did not like to clean up anymore.

When Bill went shopping,
he left the bags and boxes
all over the house.

When he had
dinner, he
let the dishes
pile up in
the kitchen.

When he went to bed,
he left his dirty clothes
lying all over the floor.

Bill could barely find a place to sit if he
wanted to read a book or watch TV.

Even his cat had trouble
finding a place to nap.

The house filled up with
more and more trash.

Soon there was so much trash in Bill's
house that it started to **bulge**. It looked
like a volcano getting ready to blow!

One day Bill's mom and dad stopped by for a visit.
"How could you let the house get so messy?" they asked.

Bill felt bad that he let things get so cluttered.
The trash was like a big bully that had taken control of
his house. It got in his way and kept him from having fun.
It was time to let the trash know that
**he** was the boss around here.

So Bill spent the entire day cleaning up the house. When he finished, he decided he should have a reward for his hard work.

That night Bill threw a big party
for himself and his friends.
They played games. They told stories.
They had cake and ice cream for dessert.
And when the party was over,
Bill and his friends cleaned up
and threw away all of the trash.

Bill's parents were proud of their son.

Bill's cat was delighted that he could sleep anywhere he wanted.

Bill was proud of himself, too.

Bill was also happy that his cat no
longer had to sleep on someone's head.

"Did you like the story?" asked Dr. Gold.

"Yes," said Ryan. "It was funny."

"Your mom and dad told me that you've been having trouble with your poops lately. Would you like to get help with those poops, so that **you** can become the boss of your body, just like Bill became the boss of his house?"

"Yes, I'd like that a lot," said Ryan.

Dr. Gold showed Ryan a picture that explained how poop is made.

"When you eat and drink, the food goes into your stomach and intestines," said Dr. Gold. "Your body then acts like a factory. It uses that food to help you grow and play and learn."

"Where does the poop come from?" asked Ryan.

"That's a good question," said Dr. Gold. "Some parts of food aren't needed. Those parts become poop."

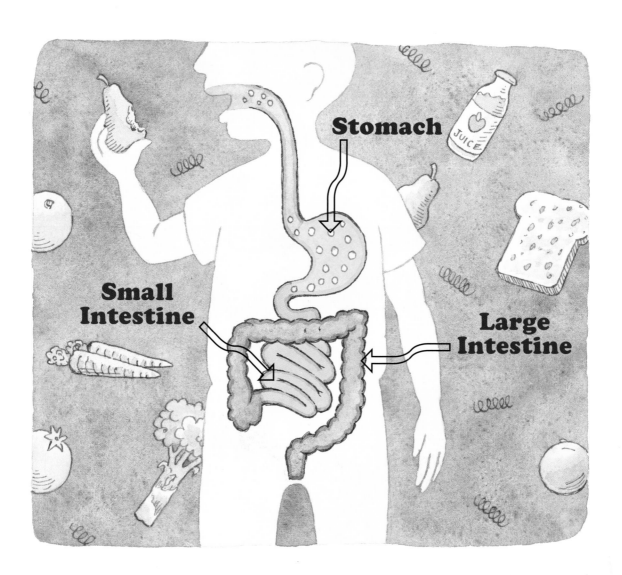

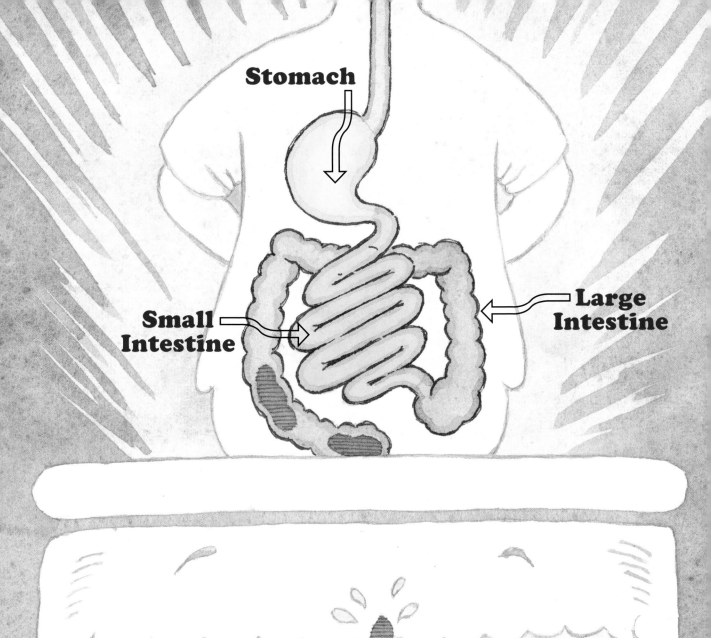

**Stomach**

**Small Intestine**

**Large Intestine**

"Poop is the trash that's left over after your body uses the food it needs. Just like Bill cleaned up his trash, people need to let the poop out of their bodies. If someone tries to hold in a poop, it won't go away. Instead, it will build up inside and cause tummy aches. Letting the poop out stops the tummy aches and makes people feel better."

"But I'm scared to let the poop out," said Ryan. "Sometimes it hurts."

"I know," said Dr. Gold. "I see lots of boys and girls who have trouble with hard poops. All of them are worried about what to do when the poop needs to come out."

"Really?" said Ryan.

"Really," said Dr. Gold.

"Wow," said Ryan. "I thought I was the only one."

"I have a plan that makes it easier for kids to poop on the potty," said Dr. Gold. "Would you like to hear about it?"

"Yes," said Ryan.

**Foods That Make Poops Softer**

FRUITS

VEGETABLES

WHOLE-GRAIN BREADS AND PASTA

WATER FRUIT JUICES

**Foods That Make Poops Harder**

CHEESE YOGURT MILK

BANANAS APPLES

WHITE BREAD AND PASTA

WHITE RICE POTATOES

"The first thing you should know is that some foods make poops softer and some foods make poops harder. What kind of foods will make it easier for you to let go of your poops? The ones that make poops softer, or the ones that make poops harder?"

"The ones that make poops softer," answered Ryan.

"Correct!" said Dr. Gold. "I knew you were a smart boy."

"Most of the time, we can stop poop problems by changing the foods that kids eat," said Dr. Gold. "And if that doesn't work, we have medicines that fix the problem."

"Can I still wear pull-ups?" asked Ryan.

"It's okay to wear them at first, if you're worried about sitting on the potty. Your parents can leave some pull-ups in the bathroom so you can put one on as soon as you know that a poop needs to come out. But once your poops are nice and soft, it will be easier if you use the potty or a regular toilet."

"Here is a plan just for you," said Dr. Gold. "It will help you fix your poop problems. We'll call it Ryan's Poop Program."

Dr. Gold gave Ryan a thumbs-up sign as he left the office. "I'll call next week to see how you are doing," she said.

"Okay," said Ryan.
"But don't be surprised if I'm
on the potty when you call!"

# Ryan's Poop Program

## 1 Watch What You Eat

Some foods make your poops bigger and harder to come out.
Other foods make your poops softer and easier to come out.
Eat more of the foods that make poops soft. Some of the foods that make poops harder are still good for you, but try to eat less of them than you used to.

### Foods That Make Poops Softer
- fruits (especially raisins, prunes, pears)
- vegetables
- pasta and bread made with whole-grain flour
- water, fruit juices (apple juice is okay)

### Foods That Make Poops Harder
- milk, cheese, yogurt
- bananas, apples
- pasta and bread made with white flour
- white rice, potatoes

## 2 Imagine How Your Poop Comes Out

Think about what is happening inside your body when you have a poop.
Some kids like to draw pictures of poop before and after it comes out.
Other kids like to use Play-Doh as pretend poop to help them understand how the poop comes out. First, put a piece of Play-Doh in a plastic bag, cut a small hole in the bag, and squeeze the Play-Doh through the hole.
Next, wet the Play-Doh with water until it gets soft and gooey.
Put the Play-Doh in the plastic bag and squeeze it through the hole.
You will find that it's easier to push out the Play-Doh when it's soft and moist. The same thing happens with poop.

## 3 Potty Practice

Sit on the potty for 5 minutes one or two times a day, even if you don't think you need to poop. By sitting on the potty, you give your body a chance to let the poop out. The best time to do this is after you eat a meal. You can bring a book or a small toy with you. Some kids like to use a timer to let them know when potty practice is over.

## 4 Keep Track of Your Poops

Make a chart with your mom or dad, and give yourself a sticker every time you have a poop. This allows you to follow your progress as your poops come out more easily.

## 5 Give Yourself a Reward
### for Becoming the Boss of Your Body

After you have been pooping regularly, give yourself a reward like Bill the Coyote did after he cleaned up his house. Here are some examples of rewards you can choose:

• a special outing with your mom or dad
• an extra book before bedtime
• you get to pick a restaurant for dinner
• a favorite dessert after dinner

# Note to Parents

by Howard J. Bennett, M.D.

*It Hurts When I Poop!* is adapted from an approach I use with patients in my pediatric practice. Although I talk about bowel habits at all well-child visits, stool problems have a way of sneaking up on people. The child who has regular poops once a day might, over a period of weeks, fall into a pattern of going two or more days without a bowel movement. Once this happens, he or she may begin holding back to avoid the pain associated with passing large stools. It is very common that adults misinterpret this behavior. Parents often tell me that their child is working hard to pass a bowel movement when he or she is actually squeezing the buttocks muscles to keep it inside.

This book is intended to help young children who are worried about going to the bathroom. Fear can be a powerful factor in a child's life, and one painful bowel movement can alter a child's confidence about what will happen when he or she tries to go. If a child learns that it is possible to have soft poops, healthy potty habits become much easier.

Changing a youngster's diet resolves toileting issues about fifty percent of the time. In many cases, you can achieve success by cutting back on constipating foods rather than asking children to eat foods they do not like. If altering the diet does not work, there are a number of medications that can help. These medicines are divided into two groups: laxatives and stool softeners. Laxatives stimulate intestinal activity, which helps propel bowel movements through the body. Stool softeners hold water in the intestinal tract, thereby making it easier to pass a stool. It is a good idea to talk to your doctor or nurse practitioner before using any medication.

*It Hurts When I Poop!* includes a "poop program" that I use with children between the ages of 3 and 6. While the program is ostensibly for Ryan, the main character in the story, my hope is that your child will want to follow these steps as well. How you approach the program will vary somewhat, depending on your child's age. Most 3- to 4-year-olds do not need to do the program in a formal way. Instead, you can incorporate parts of the program into your daily routine: Make the needed dietary changes, reward successful pooping with stickers, and consider reviewing how poops come out of the body. Most 5- to 6-year-olds are interested in doing the full program, although it is still important to be flexible. For example, if a 5-year-old does not want to do "potty practice," it is best to adjust things accordingly.

Kids love to be in charge, so it helps if you let them take the lead when you discuss the poop program. Ask them,
- "Which part of the program do you think Ryan liked best?"

- "How long do you think it took before his poops became soft?"
- "Which part of the program should we do first?"

Children may want to read the book a number of times before they are ready to work on their own issues.

Although Ryan gets stickers every time he has a poop, some children need a more enticing reward to overcome their fears. In this situation, children can be given a small treat, in addition to the sticker, when they successfully have a bowel movement. In the beginning of the program, it does not matter whether a child has bowel movements in the potty or in a pull-up. What is most important is that the child stops holding back. Encouragement for using the potty can come later.

When parents work on behavioral matters with their children, it is important to have a positive attitude and to use verbal praise whenever possible. Taking a positive approach helps children feel good about themselves; negative attitudes, even subtle ones, work against you.

If your child is unwilling to follow any of the suggestions at the end of the book, the withholding may be due to a power struggle over appropriate toileting, or he or she may have significant fears about using the potty. For example, some children are afraid they may fall into the potty. Others are frightened of the noise that happens when toilets are flushed. These situations and issues should be discussed with your doctor or nurse practitioner.

## About the Author

HOWARD J. BENNETT, M.D., practices pediatrics in Washington, D.C., and lives in Maryland with his wife and two children. He is the author of *Lions Aren't Scared of Shots* and *Waking Up Dry: A Guide to Help Children Overcome Bedwetting*. Dr. Bennett is also a clinical professor of pediatrics at the George Washington University School of Medicine and a member of the Community Advisory Staff at the Children's National Medical Center. He maintains a website (www.wakingupdry.com) where he posts information related to bedwetting.

## About the Illustrator

M.S. (MICHAEL) WEBER is a graduate of the Art Institute of Chicago. His illustrations appear in children's books and magazines, and online at Magickeys.com. "I look upon children as a new frontier," he says, "because if children are well influenced through their parents, education, and literature, the chances of our world becoming a better place will improve. This is why I illustrate children's stories." He lives in Chicago with his family.